# jubela

by CRISTINA KESSLER

illustrated by JoEllen McAllister Stammen

SIMON & SCHUSTER BOOKS FOR YOUNG READERS
NEW YORK  LONDON  TORONTO  SYDNEY  SINGAPORE

SIMON & SCHUSTER BOOKS FOR YOUNG READERS

An imprint of Simon & Schuster Children's Publishing Division

1230 Avenue of the Americas, New York, New York 10020

Text copyright © 2001 by Cristina Kessler

Illustrations copyright © 2001 by JoEllen McAllister Stammen

SIMON & SCHUSTER BOOKS FOR YOUNG READERS

is a trademark of Simon & Schuster.

Book design by Jennifer Reyes

The text of this book is set in Spectrum.

The illustrations are rendered in dry pastel on paper.

Printed in Hong Kong

10 9 8 7 6 5 4 3 2 1

Library of Congress Cataloging-in-Publication Data

Kessler, Cristina.

Jubela / by Cristina Kessler ; illustrated by JoEllen McAllister Stammen.

p. cm.    Summary: When a baby rhino loses his mother, he must rely

on his own resources to survive until he is adopted by an old female rhino.

ISBN 0-689-81895-5

1. Rhinoceroses—Juvenile fiction. [1. Rhinoceroses—Fiction. 2. Animals—

Infancy—Fiction. 3. Africa—Fiction.] I. McAllister Stammen, Jo Ellen, ill.

II. Title.

PZ10.3.K487Ju   2001

[E]—dc21   99-462170

This book is dedicated to all the park rangers, in Swaziland and everywhere else, who risk their lives everyday to save these beautiful creatures. Long live the rhinos of the world. And as always, thanks to Joe, my best friend, husband, and support system.

—C. K.


To Abba

—J. M. S.

*baby* rhino played.
He tossed and turned,
squiggled and squirmed
in the cooling mud.
His mother,
huge head hung low,
grazed nearby
to protect her baby.

Just before sunlight
surrendered to darkness,
mother scraped
the dry mud
from baby's body
with her great horn.
Baby sighed with pleasure.

*In* the African night,
mother and baby slept,
side by side.
Sudden loud bursts
ripped the night's silence.
Mother's body jolted,
then she lurched
to her feet.
She nudged baby hard
with her great horn,
then ran.

They crashed past bushes
and scrubby trees,
anthills and jagged boulders.
Baby tried to stay
at mother's side,
but it was difficult.
His short legs
had never run so far.
Or so fast.

Finally mother stopped running.
Her breathing,
ragged and troubled,
filled the air.
With a loud crash
she collapsed.
Baby dropped beside her.
Exhausted, he slept.

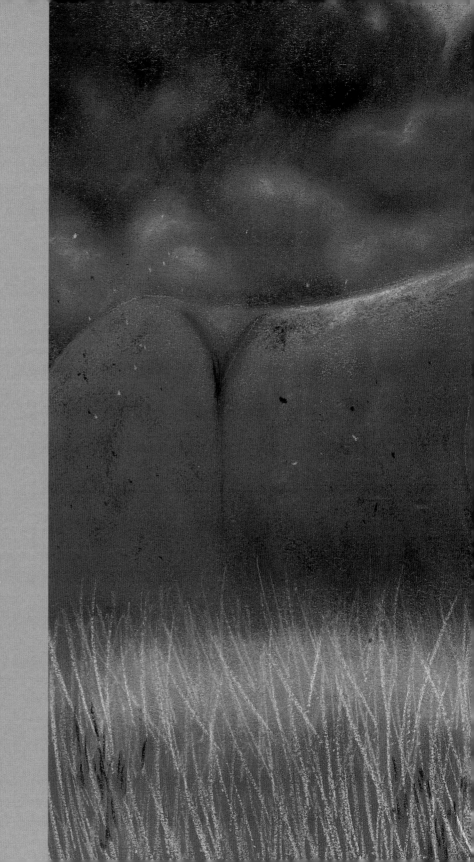

*t*he hot morning sun woke baby.
Silence greeted him.
His mother lay beside him,
but she was
oh . . . so . . . quiet.
He nudged her great head
with his square nose,
but nothing happened.
He made little noises
in her ear,
but still nothing happened.
Something was very wrong.

*a*s the sun rose
in the sky,
the temperature rose
on the land.
Heat waves danced,
and still
mother did not move
into the shade.
Baby knew at last
that mother
would never move again.

Late afternoon
found baby rhino
very hot
and very hungry.
He had no milk to drink
and was too scared
to move into
the shade alone.
He lay beside mother's
silent, still body,
completely confused.

*W*hen the African
sun slipped from sight,
coolness followed.
In the darkness,
never so big
or so black before,
baby listened to
the clicking quills
of a passing porcupine.
He was very hungry
and very thirsty
when he finally
fell asleep.

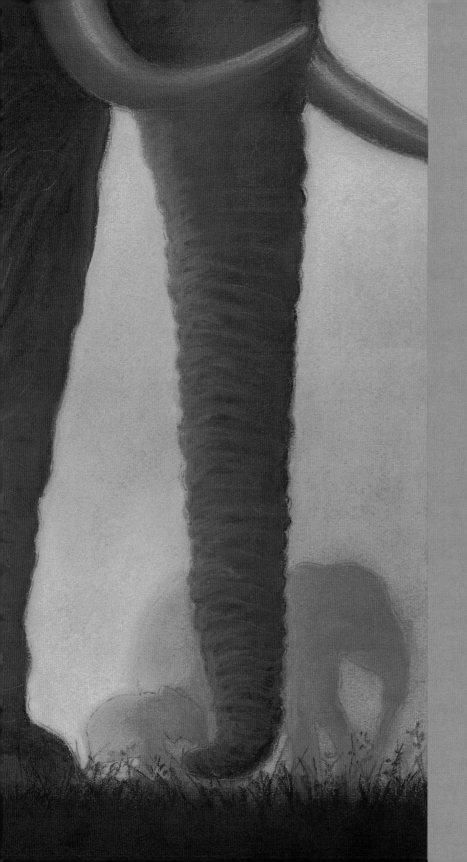

*P*assing elephants,
their long, heavy trunks
sweeping the earth,
brought the sunrise.
Not one
looked baby's way
as they passed.
Alone and afraid,
the baby stayed at his mother's side
through another
long, hot African day.

*Sunset*
and the scent of danger
arrived together.
Baby rhino rose,
poised to run.
As the smell
of man grew,
anger and terror
filled baby.

With a last look
at his dead mother,
baby ran
for the densest bush.
His clumsy feet
kicked stones aside
as he thrashed
through the thicket.
Finally he stopped,
far from the scent
of man.
Exhausted, he slept.

*Pounding* hooves
woke baby.
A herd of zebra,
running and jumping,
kicking their legs high,
enjoyed the cool
of early morning.
Baby rhino
struggled to his feet.
Slowly he followed,
for it was better
than being alone.

*h*ead down,
he trudged,
falling far behind
the frolicking herd.
When even the dust
of the zebras
disappeared,
baby collapsed
in the shade
of a tall termite hill.
He had just about
given up.

Lizards scurried,
impalas grazed,
and baby watched.
Tired.
Hungry.
And oh so thirsty.
As the day
cooled toward evening,
a new scent
floated on the air.
Quickly, he lifted
his heavy head,
smelling the breeze.
Something was coming.
Something that smelled familiar.
Something that smelled
just like mother.

baby jumped up
as a large old rhino
emerged from the bush.
Huge head hung low,
she scoured the earth
for grasses to pull
and plants to eat.

Her head snapped up
when she smelled baby's scent.
She snorted loudly.
Baby moved toward her,
but she moved her heavy head
back and forth.
Quickly, baby dropped
to the ground.

The old mother rhino
walked a wide circle
around baby.
She sniffed and snorted,
then changed directions,
walking another circle,
closer this time.
Baby remained
oh . . . so . . . still,
his head resting
on the hot ground,
frightened and hopeful
at once.

**W**ith a rub
of her wide nose,
she touched
the young rhino.
He jumped to his feet.
Starving,
he tried to nurse,
but she bumped him hard
with her side.
With little strength
and no choice,
he followed her
as she wandered
toward the setting sun.

They walked
with a far distance
between them,
for baby was tired and weak.
Old mother rhino
looked back and knew.
She slowed her pace.
She stopped
at a patch of green grass
in the shade
of an old thorn tree.
She nibbled, snuffling loudly
through her nose
as her teeth
tore grass from the ground.

*She* grazed toward baby.
She nudged his nose
with her great horn.
Baby dropped his head
and watched closely.
It did not take long
for him to follow.

He sniffed the grass,
then with his wide mouth,
he pulled some up.
Slowly he chewed.
More slowly
he swallowed.
It tasted harsh.
Nothing like mother's milk.
But its juices flowed
down his parched throat.

*t*he night passed quickly.
Old mother rhino's breathing
filled the darkness,
and her huge body,
nestled so close,
provided warmth
for the little rhino.
He slept,
knowing tomorrow
he would
eat and drink again.
And live.

*A*s days passed into
months
and months into a year,
baby rhino grew bigger
and stronger.
Old mother rhino
taught him how
to find water
and food.
He already knew,
always run from the scent
of man,
his only enemy.

Once again,
baby rhino played.
He tossed and turned,
squiggled and squirmed
in the cooling mud.
And old mother rhino,
her head hung low,
grazed nearby
to protect
her adopted son.

This book is based on a true story from Swaziland in southern Africa. Jubela, a baby rhino, actually survived the death of his mother, who was killed by poachers. A baby rhino lives on its mother's milk for one to two years, and stays close by its mother's side for four to five years. Usually, a dead mother rhino automatically means a dead baby rhino. But Jubela was lucky, for after surviving a time alone, he was adopted by an old female rhino. He was given his name, *Jubela,* which means "a fighter" in Siswati, by the park rangers at the Mkhaya Game Reserve who were impressed with his fight to survive.

Over the last thirty years, 97 percent of the world's rhino population has been lost to poachers. The International Rhino Foundation Fact Sheet reports that in 1999, the total Africa rhino population was only 11,065 rhinos. Some rhino experts have predicted the animals will be extinct in the next few years. But with an increased awareness and dedication to protecting these ancient animals, progress is being made in the fight against poachers. This is a direct result of a world concerned about the well-being of all of its creatures.